This book belongs to

SEA

Reader's Digest Children's Books

Reader's Digest Road, Pleasantville, NY 10570-7000

Copyright © 2001 Reader's Digest Children's Publishing, Inc.

Illustrations copyright © 2001 Lisa McCue

ISBN 1-57584-829-5   LC Control Number 2001 130231

10 9 8 7 6 5 4 3 2 1

Sweet Dreams

illustrated by Lisa McCue
written by L. C. Falken

Reader's Digest
Children's Books

Pleasantville, New York • Montréal, Québec

One warm summer day, three little bunnies
played in the garden all day long.

They were still outside when the sun began
to set and the fireflies came out to play, too.

The screen door opened and Mama Bunny called,
"Time to come inside, my little bunnies. Dinner is ready."
"Can't we stay outside just a little longer?"
asked Rosy. "Please?"
"I'm not hungry yet," said Posy.
"Dinner, dinner, what's for dinner?" asked Dozy.
"Come and see," said Mama.

The three little bunnies washed their paws and faces. Then they sat down to a scrumptious dinner.

They had spicy carrot stew (that was Rosy's favorite),
crispy lettuce salad (that was Dozy's favorite), and lots
of fresh munchy, crunchy radishes (which Posy liked
more than anything else).

After dinner, the bunnies went out on the porch.
Mama sat in her rocker, sipping sweet clover tea.
Rosy, Posy, and Dozy sat on the steps and looked at
the stars sparkling high above.
"Look," Posy cried. "A shooting star!"
"Wish, wish, make a wish!" said Dozy.

"You can make one, too," said Rosy. "But you
mustn't tell your wish or it might not come true."
Then the three little bunnies watched as the big
bright moon rose up in the sky.
"Time to get ready for bed now," Mama said softly.

"Bubbles, bubbles, I want bubbles!" cried Dozy.
Rosy poured in some bubble bath while Mama
made sure the water was just right for her three
little bunnies.

The tub filled up with warm, bubbly water and they all hopped in.

When the bunnies were clean and dry and had their pajamas on, Mama said, "Don't forget to brush your teeth."

"Then can we have a story?" asked Posy.
"Please?" said Rosy.
"Please, please, pretty please?" said Dozy.
"Of course," said Mama with a smile.

Mama sat on the sofa and Rosy, Posy, and Dozy snuggled up close.

"Read us the story about the bunny who runs away," said Posy.

Mama did. Then Rosy said, "What if we ran away?"

"Would you come and find us?" asked Posy.

"Yes, I would," Mama said. "I'd find each one of you no matter where you were, and I'd bring you all right back home with me."

"Look, Mama," Rosy whispered. "Dozy's asleep."

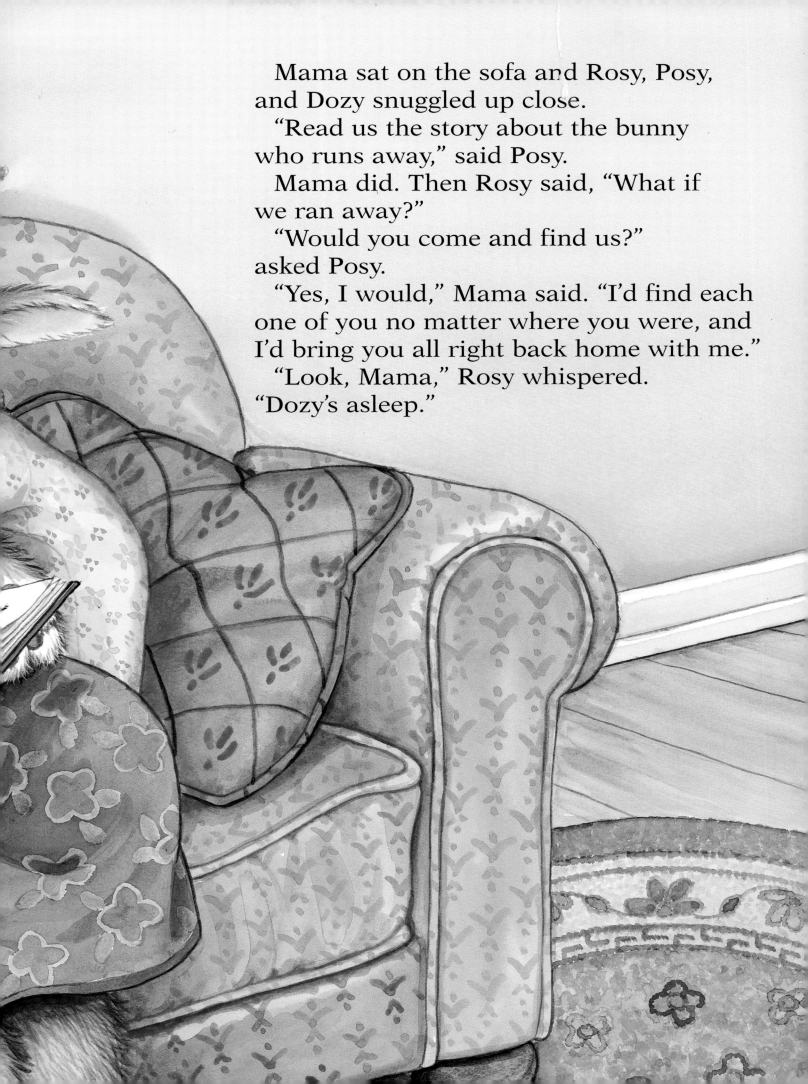

Mama carried Dozy to the bedroom. Then she tucked all three of her little bunnies into bed. "Good night, my little ones," she said. "I love you."

"We love you, too," Rosy and Posy said.

Dozy mumbled, "Love, love, Mama love," in his sleep.

Mama turned off the light.
"Sleep tight, my little bunnies,"
she whispered. "May you have
sweet dreams all through
the night."